PUFFIN BOOKS

SOS for Rita

Also by Hilda Offen

HAPPY CHRISTMAS, RITA!

In Puffin picture books

ELEPHANT PIE
NICE WORK, LITTLE WOLF!

Other titles in the First Young Puffin series

SOS for Rita

Written and illustrated by
Hilda Offen

PUFFIN BOOKS

PUFFIN BOOKS

Published by the Penguin Group
Penguin Books Ltd, 27 Wrights Lane, London W8 5TZ, England
Penguin Books USA Inc., 375 Hudson Street, New York, New York 10014, USA
Penguin Books Australia Ltd, Ringwood, Victoria, Australia
Penguin Books Canada Ltd, 10 Alcorn Avenue, Toronto, Ontario, Canada M4V 3B2
Penguin Books (NZ) Ltd, 182–190 Wairau Road, Auckland 10, New Zealand

Penguin Books Ltd, Registered Offices: Harmondsworth, Middlesex, England

First published by Hamish Hamilton Ltd 1992
Published in Puffin Books 1995
5 7 9 10 8 6

Text and illustrations copyright © Hilda Offen, 1992
All rights reserved

The moral right of the author/illustrator has been asserted

Manufactured in China by Imago Publishing

The Potter children were excited. It was the first day of their holiday.

"Can we go to the beach now, Mum?" asked Eddie.

"Yes," called Mrs Potter from inside the caravan. "But take care of Rita – she's only little."

"Oh no!" groaned Eddie, Julie and Jim.

They set off down the cliff path, and Rita
trotted along behind.

"Why have you brought that old box?"
asked Jim.

"What a silly thing to bring to the beach," said Julie.

Rita kept quiet. "If only they knew what's inside!" she thought.

They reached the beach and looked along the sands.

"I'm going swimming," said Eddie.

"I'm going for a donkey-ride," said Julie.

"I'm going on the helter-skelter," said Jim.

"You can look after our towels, Rita," they shouted as they ran off.

Rita watched them
disappear.

"Oh well, I'll do a
spot of sunbathing,"
she said, sitting down.

She'd hardly closed
her eyes when along
the beach came the
Bertram brothers.
Their ball landed on
Rita's towel.

"Out of the way,
titch!" said Billy.

"Oops! Sorry!"
said Boris,
pretending to miss
the ball, and he
kicked sand

all over Rita.

"Just you wait!"
thought Rita, but she
had no time to feel
cross.

A scream rang out
along the beach. Julie's
donkey had bolted
and was heading
for the rocks!

"This is a job for the
Rescuer!" said Rita,
grabbing her
special box.

"Where can I change?" she wondered. "I
know – the Punch and Judy stall."

In a split second she had put on her
Rescuer outfit. She was ready for action!

"Help!" screamed Julie, clinging on to the donkey's neck.

Rita raced after them like an Olympic sprinter. She grasped the donkey's reins and leaped onto its back.

"Whoa!" she cried, and the donkey skidded to a halt.

"You've saved my little Neddy!" gasped Mr Khan, puffing up behind them.

"And me too!" cried Julie. "Can I have your autograph, please, Rescuer?"

"Another time, perhaps," said Rita, who had spotted more trouble. "I think I'm needed over there."

Mr Muscles, the Strong Man from the
pier, had fallen into the quicksands! And so
had the rest of the Muscles family! They
had been watching a plane doing aerobatics
and had been looking up when they should
have been looking down.

Mr Muscles had sunk up to his chin, Mrs
Muscles up to her armpits, Grandma
Muscles up to her waist, and little Mervin
Muscles up to his knees.

"Help!" they cried.

14

"Hold on to this!" cried Rita, flying over to them with an oar.

What a good thing Mr Muscles had a strong set of teeth!

"One-two-three-pull!" cried Rita.

Squelch! Slurp! Glug! Pop! – out shot the Muscles family.

"How can we ever repay you?" gasped Mr Muscles, emptying sand from his pockets. But Rita was already zooming off towards the helter-skelter. Jim had been trying to do a headstand on his coconut mat and had shot over the side.

"He'll be killed!" cried the people on the ground.

"Not if I can help it," said Rita, and she flashed through the air at the speed of light.

"Ooh!" gasped the crowd, and "Well-held!" they cried as Rita caught Jim in her arms and set him down safely on the pavement.

"Can't stop!" said Rita.

She had spotted someone else in trouble.
Far out on the horizon, a seagull was
pecking at Mrs Miller's lilo.

Whoosh! The air rushed out and the lilo
started to sink.

"Help!" screamed Mrs Miller.

Rita came skimming over the waves.

"Hang on!" she cried, and she dived into
the sea. With three giant puffs she blew the
lilo up again. She stuck her finger in the
puncture and pushed Mrs Miller back to the
beach.

As she stepped ashore, Rita heard someone crying. The Bertram brothers were kicking down Tommy Tiler's sandcastle.

"I've had enough of you!" said Rita. She grasped the bullies by their shirts and whisked them away. Then she hung them from the top of the windsock.

"Help!" screamed Boris and Billy; but no one took any notice.

"That's one rescue I *won't* be doing,"
said Rita, and she helped Tommy build the
biggest sandcastle on the beach.

But Rita's work was not over yet! Out at
sea something else was happening. The
swimmers splashed around in panic as a
dark fin cut through the water.

"Shark!" screamed Eddie, who was
directly in its path. "Help!"

"Here I come!" cried Rita, and she seized
a coil of rope.

Rita dived down and knotted the rope round the shark's jaw.

"Now you can't bite anyone," she said.

The shark was furious. It thrashed its
tail, it leaped out of the water, it rolled and
it dived, but it could not shake Rita off its
back. Soon it was completely exhausted.

"Do you promise to go away if I untie you?" asked Rita.

The shark nodded, so Rita untied the knot.

"Off you go!" she said. The shark could hardly wait to make its escape. It would never go near another beach again.

"Hooray for the Rescuer!" cried the
people on the shore. "Hip-hip-hooray!"
They clapped and cheered, and they rushed
forward and gave Rita ice-cream and
candyfloss and lollipops.

"Thank you," said Rita, and ate them
all up.

"Now I need some exercise," she said.

First she headed a beach ball up and
down for half an hour. Then she swam ten
times between the two piers.

"You can have three thousand free
bounces on my Bouncing Castle," said Mr
Robinson. "And you can keep your boots
on!"

Rita bounced and bounced and bounced until a clock struck seven.

"Time to change!" said Rita, and she slipped back to the Punch and Judy stall.

"Where have you been?" cried Eddie, when Rita arrived back at the caravan. "We looked everywhere for you."

"Didn't you see the Rescuer?" asked Julie.

"She wrestled with a shark!" cried Jim.

"What were you doing?" asked Eddie.

"Oh – just this and that!" said Rita, and she tucked the box under her bunk.

Also available in First Young Puffin

BLESSU
Dick King-Smith

The tall, flowering elephant-grasses give Blessu hayfever. 'BLESS YOU!' all the elephants cry whenever little Blessu sneezes, which is very often. Blessu grows slowly except for one part of him – his trunk – and his sneeze becomes the biggest, loudest sneeze in the world!

WHAT STELLA SAW
Wendy Smith

Stella's mum is a fortune teller who always gets things wrong. But when football-mad Stella starts reading tea-leaves, she seems to be right every time! Or is she . . .

THE DAY THE SMELLS WENT WRONG
Catherine Sefton

It is just an ordinary day, but Jackie and Phil can't understand why nothing smells as it should. Toast smells like tar, fruit smells like fish, and their school dinners smell of perfume! Together, Jackie and Phil discover the cause of the problem . . .